P9-CLE-271

ANN MORRIS

FAMILIES

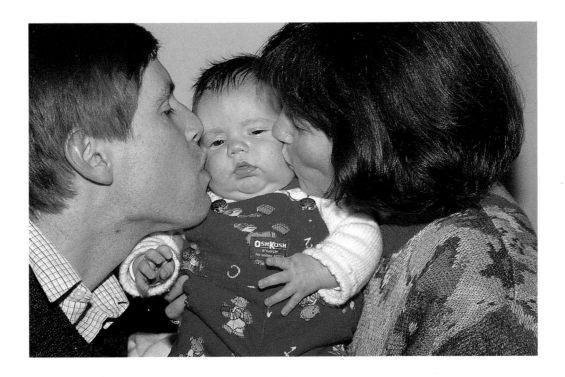

HarperCollins**Publishers**

The author wishes to thank the following for the use of their photographs: front jacket—© Martha Cooper/The Viesti Collection; pp. 1, 17, back jacket—© Nancy Durrell McKenna/The Hutchison Library; p. 3—© Peter Linenthal; p. 4—© Betty Press/Woodfin Camp & Associates; pp. 5 (left), 7, 9 (right), 12 (left), 14 (right), 21, 29 (left)—© George Ancona; pp. 5 (right), 28 (right)—© John Eastcott/Yva Momatiuk/Woodfin Camp & Associates; p. 6—© Catherine Karnow/ Woodfin Camp & Associates; pp. 8, 22 (right), 25 (left and right), 26 (left)—© Ellen B. Senisi; pp. 9 (left), 14 (left), 22 (left), 23(left), 24 (top)—© Ken Heyman/Woodfin Camp & Associates; p. 10—© Paul Chesley/Tony Stone Images; p. 11—© Stephanie Maze/Woodfin Camp & Associates; p. 12 (middle)—© Elliott Smith/International Stock; p. 12 (right)—© Eric A. Wessman/Viesti Associates, Inc.; pp. 13, 16 (right)—© Michal Heron/Woodfin Camp & Associates; p. 15—© Tom Stoddart/Katz/Woodfin Camp & Associates; p. 16 (left)—© James Wilson/Woodfin Camp & Associates; p. 18—© Leland Bobbe/Tony Stone Images; p. 19—© Lawrence Migdale/Tony Stone Images; p. 20 (left)—© Scott Barrow/International Stock; p. 20 (right)—© Ann Morris; p. 23 (right)—© Mark Bolster/International Stock; p. 24 (bottom)—© A. Ramey/Woodfin Camp & Associates; p. 26 (right)—© Zigy Kaluzny/Tony Stone Images; p. 27—© Mike Yamashita/Woodfin Camp & Associates; p. 28 (left)—© Frank Priegue/International Stock; p. 29 (middle)—© Nubar Alexanian/Woodfin Camp & Associates; p. 29 (right)—©Andrew Hill/The Hutchison Library.

Families
Text copyright © 2000 by Ann Morris
Manufactured in China by South China Printing Company Ltd.
All rights reserved.
http://www.harperchildrens.com

Library of Congress Cataloging-in-Publication Data
Morris, Ann.
Families/by Ann Morris.
p. cm.
Summary: A simple explanation of families, how they function, how they are different, and how they are alike.
ISBN 0-688-17198-2 (trade)—ISBN 0-688-17199-0 (library)
1. Family—Juvenile literature. [1. Family.] I. Title.
HQ744.M67 2000 306.85—dc21 99-37036 CIP

19 20
❖

Curr
HQ
744
.M67
2000

FAMILIES

Everyone,

everywhere,

is part of a family.

People in families love and care for one another...

even on bad days.

9

They help one another.

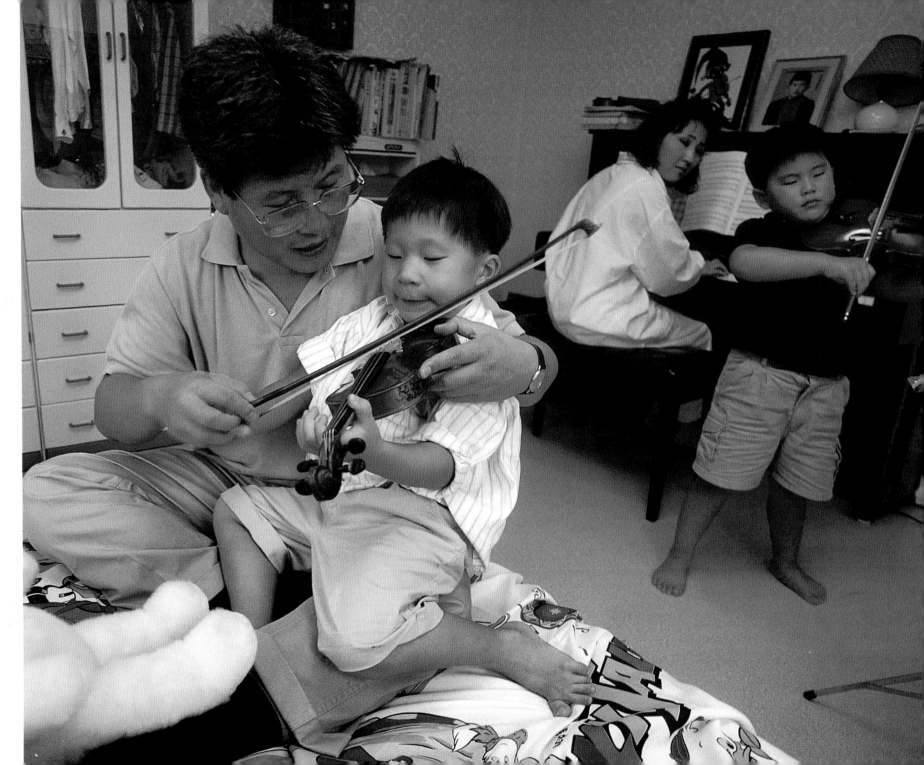

They work together.

They play together.

They cook

and eat . . .

and celebrate together.

Families come in all sizes.
Some children have many brothers and sisters.
Others have none.

Some children have lots of aunts and uncles and cousins.
Others have fewer.

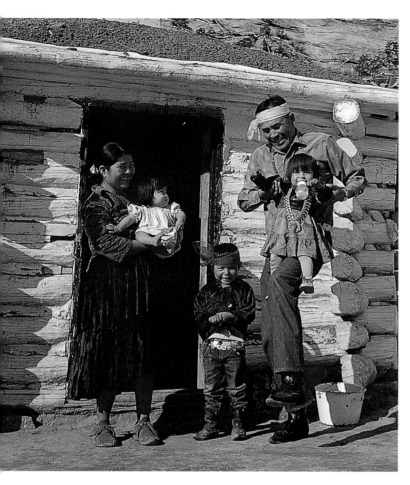

Some children
live with their mothers
and fathers.

Others have stepparents
or live with just
one parent.

Some children live with a grandparent or a foster family.
Others are adopted by parents who chose them specially.

25

But all children are
part of families.

Whether you go to lands near or far,
families are there—big and small,

loving, sharing,
and caring—

wherever you are.

INDEX

16 UNITED STATES: Making tacos with Mom in San Antonio, Texas.

17 CANADA: Everyone loves corn on the cob.

18 UNITED STATES: A Passover seder in Long Island, New York, brings several generations together.

19 UNITED STATES: In Sacramento, California, making skull masks for the Day of the Dead festival.

20 RUSSIA: A family on a rainy day at Red Square in Moscow.

21 UNITED STATES: The entire family gathers to sing "Happy 100th Birthday" to Grandma Craig in La Junta, Colorado.

22 UNITED STATES: A Navajo family outside its log hogan in Monument Valley, Arizona.

22 UNITED STATES: A family at home in Schenectady, New York.

23 UNITED STATES: A Pittsburgh, Pennsylvania, father and son painting fishing lures.

24 UNITED STATES: These toddlers in Los Angeles, California, are much loved by their foster parents.

25 UNITED STATES: A mother reads with her adopted Korean son in upstate New York.

27 JAPAN: Capturing a family picnic on video in Tokyo.

28 CANADA: This grandpa in the Hutterite colony in Pincher Creek, Alberta, smiles lovingly at his two-week-old granddaughter.

29 UNITED STATES: Camping with the family in Harriman State Park, New York, is lots of fun.

29 UNITED STATES: Getting ready for church in San Marcos, Texas.

29 INDIA: A family out for a walk in Rhanikhet, North India.

Where in the world were these photographs taken?

PACIFIC
OCEAN

NORTH
AMERICA

Canada

United States

ATLANTIC
OCEAN

Puerto Rico
(United States)

CENTRAL AMERICA

Brazil

SOUTH AMERICA

United
Kingdom

EUROPE

Russia

ASIA

AFRICA

Saudi
Arabia

India

Ethiopia

Vietnam

Japan

South Korea

PACIFIC
OCEAN

INDIAN
OCEAN

AUSTRALIA